Our Cat Henry
Comes to the Swings

For all the children at Meadow Lane   K.C. and J.B.

OXFORD
UNIVERSITY PRESS

Great Clarendon Street, Oxford OX2 6DP

Oxford University Press is a department of the University of Oxford.
It furthers the University's objective of excellence in research, scholarship,
and education by publishing worldwide in

Oxford New York

Auckland Bangkok Buenos Aires Cape Town Chennai
Dar es Salaam Delhi Hong Kong Istanbul Karachi Kolkata
Kuala Lumpur Madrid Melbourne Mexico City Mumbai Nairobi
São Paulo Shanghai Taipei Tokyo Toronto

Oxford is a registered trade mark of Oxford University Press
in the UK and in certain other countries

Text copyright © Kate Clanchy 2005
Illustrations copyright © Jemima Bird 2005

First published 2005

British Library Cataloguing in Publication Data available

ISBN 0 19 279122 2 Hardback
ISBN 0 19 272557 2 Paperback

10 9 8 7 6 5 4 3 2 1

Printed in China

For Lauren + Jack

Our Cat Henry
Comes to the Swings

Kate Clanchy and Jemima Bird

Kate Clanchy

Jemima Bird

OXFORD

UNIVERSITY PRESS

When we go to the swings in the afternoon
our cat Henry comes along too.

Henry - cats don't
come for walks.

I ride my trike. Our Henry stalks the walls and

the gaps, and clambers low,

paw
over
paw,

to follow the flying yellow leaves

and sprints with ease past Mrs Perkins's Pekinese,

and cross Next Door's two cross borzois. In a single

furry bound he dashes round the
basset-hound, leaves the Labrador in a heap of

leaves and leads the dachshund with the e-l-a-s-

-tic lead
round my trike,
three trees,
my friend Mike's new orange bike,

through the park-keeper's great big
rake and all his raked-up bonfire sticks

right to the playground gate.

H goes under.
We go through.
No Dogs!
How true.

Henry's safe inside.
He presides at
the slide.

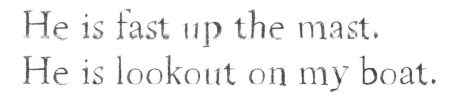

He is fast up the mast.
He is lookout on my boat.

Henry, king of all the swings.

Time to go back home for tea.
We say bye-bye to Mrs P, and 'Scuse me, please!'
to the borzois and the Pekinese.

We confound the basset-hound.
We nip round the knotted-up dachshund.

We're nearly
at our own
back door
when we
meet the
Labrador.
Big eyes.
Big paws.

BIG
pause.

Then Henry flies - I *knew* he could -

straight
for the gate

and our kitchen door. SLAM

Dogs out.

Us in.

Mum and me and him.

Henry, don't do that again.

Henry, the cat who comes to the swings.